Life as a Doctor Mom

written by
Lauren Hayward, MD

illustrated by
Cheryl Souch

Twitter: @DoctorMomLife
Facebook: @DoctorMomLife
Instagram: DoctorMomLife

Tellwell Talent
www.tellwell.ca

ISBN
978-1-77302-605-3 (Paperback)

Dedication

To Alistair

Being a doctor is fun, but being your mom
is the best gig in the world.

Maureen,

Words can't express how much we appreciate all the work you put into moving us. Even though it may not seem like we do! lol

We love you from the bottom of our hearts

Giles & Lenox

Acknowledgments

The following people gave me inspiration and encouragement to skip charting, order takeout and write this book.

To my husband Jeremy. Thanks for taking part in making Alistair. Thanks also for strong coffee, delicious meals, excellent back rubs and your impeccable sense of humour that comes out best when I don't feel like laughing. Thank you for putting up with the craziness that comes with being married to a rural family doctor. Thank you for the sweet, sweet naps that you allow me to take on my post-call days whilst wrangling our toddler.

To Cheryl. You are an amazing artist, but above all, you are a woman with a heart of gold. I am so honoured that you agreed to share in this book-writing journey. Thank you for magically transforming the scrambled ideas that I had in my head into creative, beautiful images.

To my family. Mama, papa, Amy, Jenna, Matt, Craig, Layton and Blake. I'm not sure how I got so lucky to be surrounded by such astounding relatives. You have been there through the good and the bad moments as I slugged through training and establishing my practice, and now as a mom. I continue to appreciate the love, support, hugs and laughs. Mama, thanks for the gross stories around the dinner table from your nursing shifts in the ER, which helped inspire me to become a doctor. Now I get to tell gross stories too!

To my in-law family. (Yeah, I love them. I really struck gold on the in-law front.) Mark, Gail, Amanda, Jennifer, Sydney and Christian. I know where Jeremy gets his kindness, thoughtfulness and selflessness from. I hope that, together, Jeremy and I can pass these important qualities on to Alistair. Thank you for welcoming me into your family and for always being there for us.

To my amazing colleagues in Listowel. My fellow physicians Arif, Barb, Derek, Evelyn, Gill, Greg, Lisa, Paul, Terry, Ravi, Rex, Rob and Russell, our awesome locums, and all of the staff at the clinic and hospital (and your families). I wake up most mornings feeling like I won the work lottery. (That day when I got sprayed in the face by a whole bottle of activated charcoal in the ER was an exception.) You inspire, uplift and support me. Medicine is a team sport, and I have the best team possible. To those of you who are moms, thank you for the camaraderie, mentorship and baby stuff. As I've learned from you, "I have a messy house and a happy family."

To my best friends and to my Comfort Zone. You know who you are, and you have had a huge part in shaping me into the person I am today. Even though I don't see some of you often, the time we do get together is so cherished. Thank goodness for group texts, especially at 3:00 a.m. while dealing with our babies or with patients. Those ungodly-hour moments are way less lonely because of you.

To my fellow Canadian doctor moms and other physician moms everywhere. I draw strength, reassurance and knowledge from your stories and your questions. You are one hell of a hive that I feel honoured to be a part of. I hope that this book can provide some laughs after the tough days. Feel free to pair it with wine and online shopping.

To my patients, who continuously challenge me to be a good doctor and to find a balance in life. Having the privilege and responsibility of being so closely involved in your lives is not a duty that I take lightly. If providing good care means having a perpetual six-foot heap of laundry at home and only emptying my bladder once in twelve hours some days, I'll take it.

To all of the other doctors in various towns and hospitals with whom I have had the pleasure of working, and to those who have taught, mentored and inspired me along the way– thank you.

Cheryl's Acknowledgments

I would like to thank my husband Gary for supporting me in my crazy ventures even if he's not involved. Thank you to my children Melissa, Mathew, Felicia, Laura, Xavier and Keeara, who join me on my crazy ventures when their dad doesn't. Thank you to my parents Ralph and Sharon Darlow. You are the reason I am who I am. Thank you to my crazy sisters Darlene and Nancy. We support each other, we love each other, and we fight with each other! Thank you to the many teachers who uplifted me along my bumpy path.

Foreword by Jenna Harron and Amy Jakubaitis (Lauren's Sisters)

As a newlywed, a new homeowner and a newly minted doctor, life was going quite smoothly for Lauren. She wore sharply tailored outfits to work. She went to the gym regularly. She filled her spare time with relaxing dinners with friends and watching movies with her husband, Jeremy. After the mayhem of her medical training, Lauren was finally enjoying the freedom of holidays, taking up new hobbies, and an active social life.

Her doctor colleagues with kids sometimes seemed like a hot mess. They would show up late to meetings, limping because they had tripped on some toy that their kid had left on the floor. They had stickers stuck in their hair and they wore mismatched socks. They would whip out a maple-syrup-covered tablet from their diaper-filled purse. Did having kids thrust these ladies' lives into a state of chaos?

Lauren wondered what she would be like when she had kids. Would she coordinate her socks? Would she remember to bring her own lasagna lunch to work and not the baby's carrot puree? Would she make time to exercise and at least shower daily?

Absolutely, she would.

And then Lauren had her own baby.

And those stickers in her colleagues' hair finally made sense to her.

She went from being fifteen minutes early to everything, to arriving anywhere from two to forty-three minutes late. Her tailored work outfits morphed into yoga shirts with breast milk seeping through them. (It's a damn good thing that blanket scarves were in style!) She threw a party when she managed to have three hot, uninterrupted showers in a week. She forgot how to spell Amoxicillin and the name for "that infectious sore throat thing" (and later remembered that it's called "Strep"). She got dressed in the dark – couldn't risk waking up the baby – and grabbed any socks she could find. Who cares if they matched or if they were Jeremy's socks that were three sizes too big! She would rush out of the house in the morning and absentmindedly swing her "stethoscope" over her shoulder, realizing only when she arrived at work that it was actually her son's homemade noodle necklace, which is damn near useless at picking up murmurs.

While sitting at the dinner table one Tuesday night with Jeremy, eating cold leftover macaroni and cheese at 9:00 p.m., Lauren took off her baggy socks and dusted herself off...literally; her son had managed to bite off the top of a bottle of baby powder, covering her in what looked like a thin layer of dust. On the plus side, her new, young colleague saw this dust and thought that she was so accomplished for tackling home renovations with a baby. Bless this rookie, she had no idea! Lauren realized that this chaos was now her everyday life, toy-car-induced limp and all, and that she could now really relate to her fellow doctor moms. Rather than fighting the chaos, she figured she might as well embrace it and find the humour in it. What better way to laugh at her experiences than to collect them in a book for other doctor moms to enjoy!

So, ladies, forget charting or tidying the house. Instead, try to sit back (if you can find room amongst the toys and mystery splotches on the couch) and take delight in some of the familiar moments experienced as a doctor mom. And, remember that you've got a whole tribe of other moms with stickers in their hair and maple syrup on their tablets who know just what you're going through.

A mandatory purchase for any Dr. Mom's baby shower: the mini-doctor outfit. She usually receives several of them.

Dr. Mom is good at denying the fact that she, herself, may be going into labour.

Baby's first book. Dr. Mom saved this one from medical school, because memorizing the brachial plexus takes awhile and she wants the baby to get a head start.

True story.

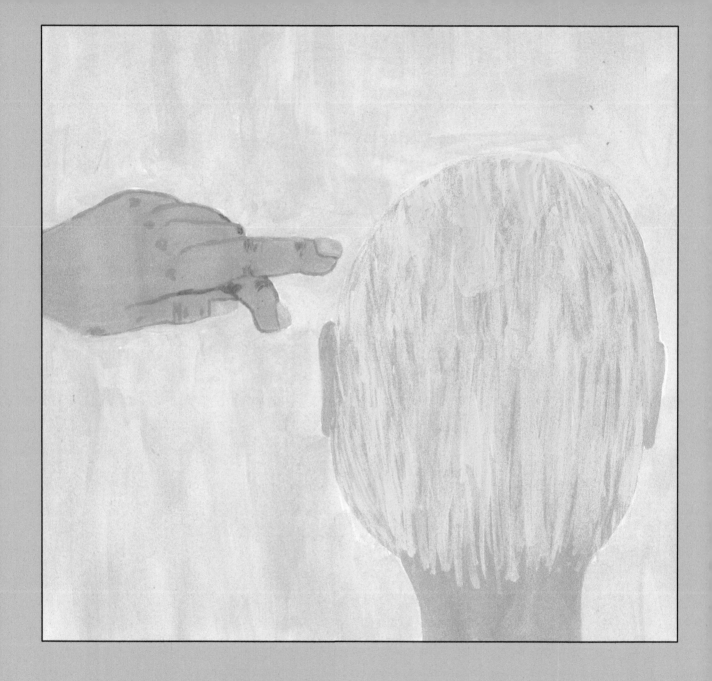

Must...not...pick...off...baby's...cradle...cap.

How a breastfeeding Dr. Mom studies for exams. Oh, the irony.

Anatomy of Dr. Mom's bookshelf.

Why do fast-food restaurants use medication administration cups for their ketchup?

Baby's first fever.

"Dear Call Karma: If you could give me four hours of uninterrupted sleep during this shift, that would be better than what I'm getting at home with the kids. In fact, it would almost feel like a holiday."

(Like that would ever actually happen.)

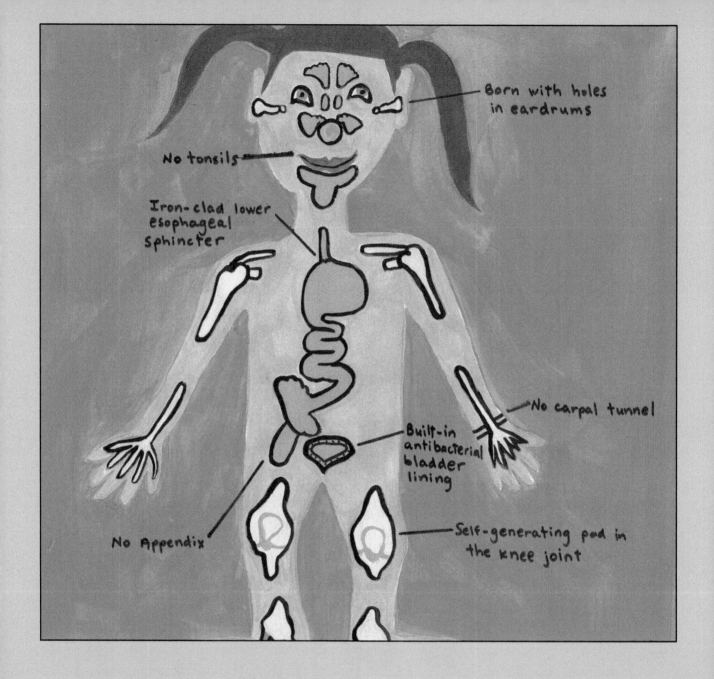

Dr. Mom fantasizes about changing the body to make work less onerous.

Dr. Mom smells like pee. She's not sure whether it's from work or from her baby's diaper explosion.

Dr. Mom is either the best, or the most annoying,
friend to have when you're pregnant.

Dr. Mom will never look at baby powder the same way again after pulling a bottle of it out of a man's rectum the other day.

Baby's first (and second) casual exposures to peanut butter.

Old textbooks are also very useful for supporting stubby baby legs.

Speaking of friends having babies, forget cute clothes and fun toys. Dr. Mom is queen of the practical baby gift.

The rare child-free, work-free getaway begins. And then, Dr. Mom hears this...

Friday afternoon Operating Room footwear. It's almost Happy Hour!

Mystery splotches.

Dr. Mom's three-minute "working lunch"...

At least she gets to eat, right?

Even in the most romantic of moments, patients are on Dr. Mom's mind.

Grocery store abbreviations make for a delicious end-of-life care plan.

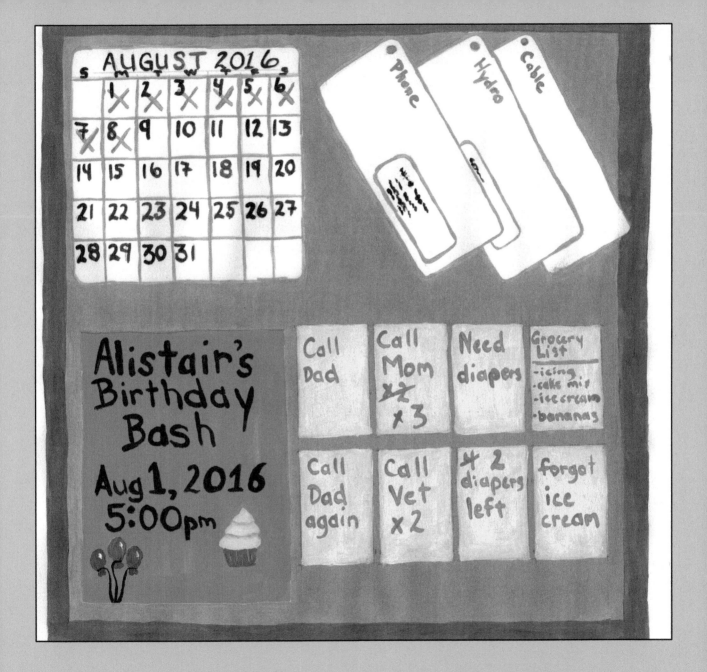

Dr. Mom has committed 310 clinical practice guidelines to memory but forgets her four-item grocery list. And her son's first birthday.

Hobbies... What are those again? Does charting count?

Blue Popsicle residue is easily mistaken for cyanosis. This is especially scary when the kid is already fevered and snotty.

Petroleum jelly goes well on everything! Diaper rashes, dry skin...

As well as the TV and the dog, apparently.

A typical day's to-do list.

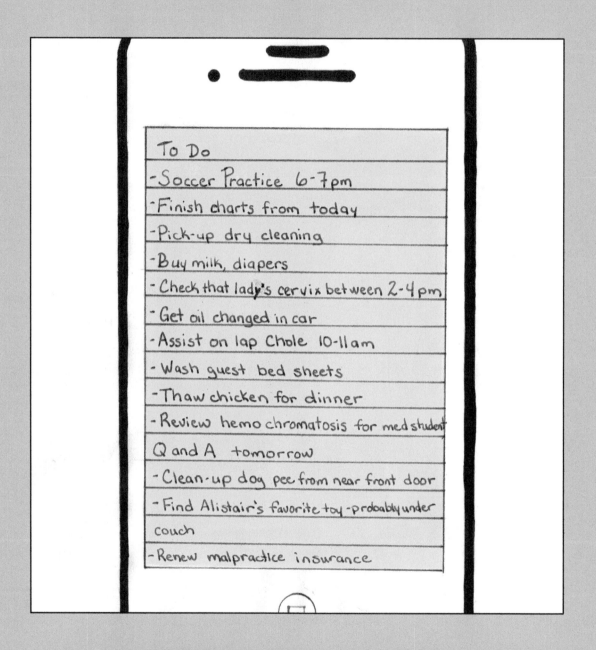

(That dog pee will probably still be there tomorrow.)

What studying for licensing exams with a toddler looks like.

After a long workday, Dr. Mom just needs a little glass of wine to decompress.

Why buy needles and thread?

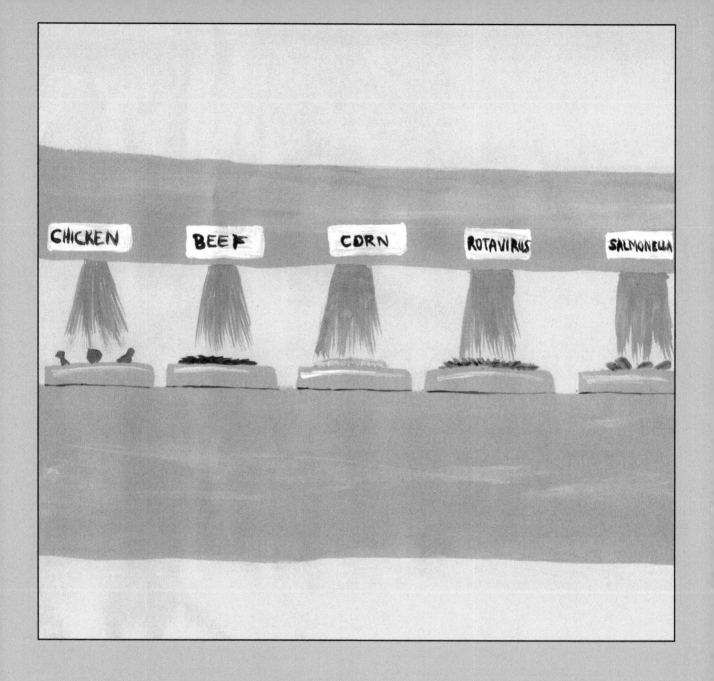

Food is not the only thing Dr. Mom sees on the menu at the buffet.

The essential 'sick kid corner' at the office, for all of those work
days when Dr. Mom's barfing child is banned from school.

Bake Day at school...

Dr. Mom isn't quitting her day job anytime soon.

Dr. Mom is always questioning the evidence.

The struggle is real.

Dr. Mom isn't known for giving out the coolest Halloween treats,
but she always has stuff lying around to make cool costumes.

This usually occurs after fifteen minutes of Dr. Mom introducing herself and discussing the treatment plan.

A routine "quick" pit stop before heading to
the park on Saturday mornings...

"Quick" is usually a lie.

A romantic dinner with the hubby.

Counting sheep to fall asleep does not work for Dr. Mom.

Road-trip entertainment. Fun for the whole family! Or not.

When the forecast calls for snow...

A Saturday afternoon at the rink isn't complete without a question about haemorrhoids from Hockey Mom.

Christmas Card Mailing List

Jenna	Amanda	Matthew
Gail	Kathy	Jennifer
Amy	Jeremy	Ray
Craig	Mark	Sydney
Georgia	Avery	Liam
Kaden	(Melena)	Carter
Layton	Ethan	Jackson
Pippa	Lukas	William
Norah	Connor	Gabrielle
Blake	Keeara	Xavier
Laura	Felicia	Zachary
Mathew	Melissa	Hailey
Sébastien	Owen	Edyn
Christian	Caleb	Sophie
Abby	Aeson	Colin
Leah	Lily	Emerson
Kamden	Alexandra	Olivia
Hannah	Whitney	Bennett

www.StickyPaperPadYouGotForFreeAtSomeConference.ca

Dr. Mom thinks to herself, "I wonder if her parents knew the medical definition of that word when they named her that."

Can you spot Dr. Mom enjoying her kid's school play?

Must-have decor. Christmas DOES fall right in the
middle of cold and flu season, after all.

A relaxing beach vacation.

Exciting indeed.

Dr. Mom's lingo can be confusing.

Dr. Mom is dedicated to making healthy meals for
her kids, yet this is her lunch most days.

Three little monkeys jumping on the bed
One fell off and bumped his head
Mama IS the doctor and the doctor said:

Dr. Mom keeps it simple.

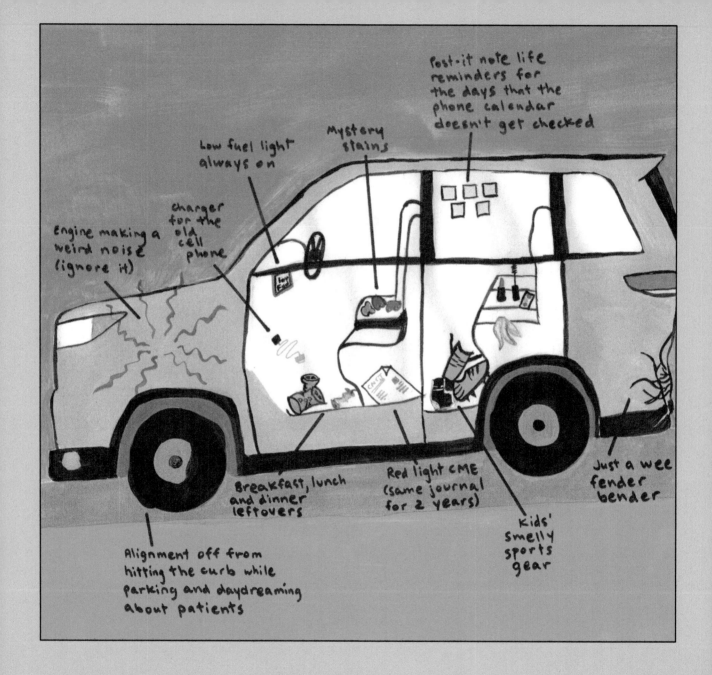

Anatomy of Dr. Mom's car.

Saving on veterinary bills.

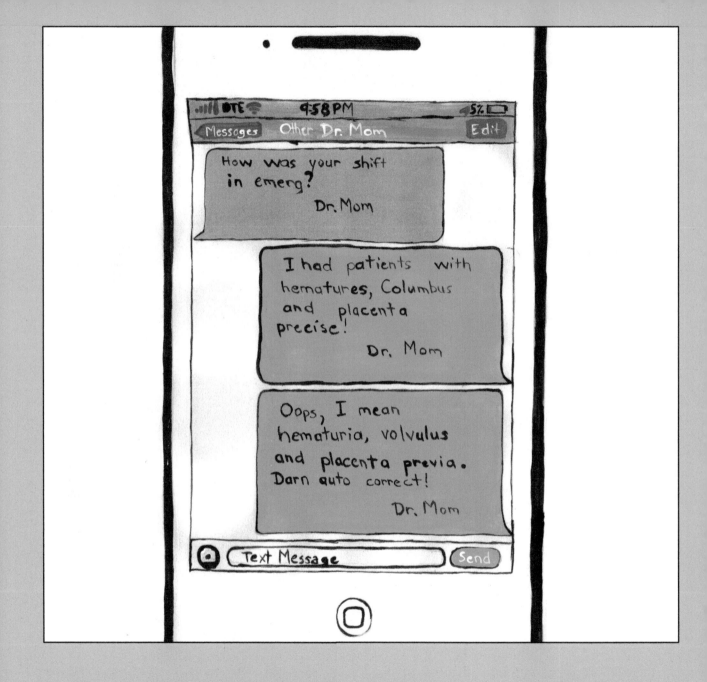

Autocorrect, Dr. Mom style.

What's considered to be the height of style for Dr. Mom is
quite different than what's on the fashion runways.

He is definitely a doctor's child.

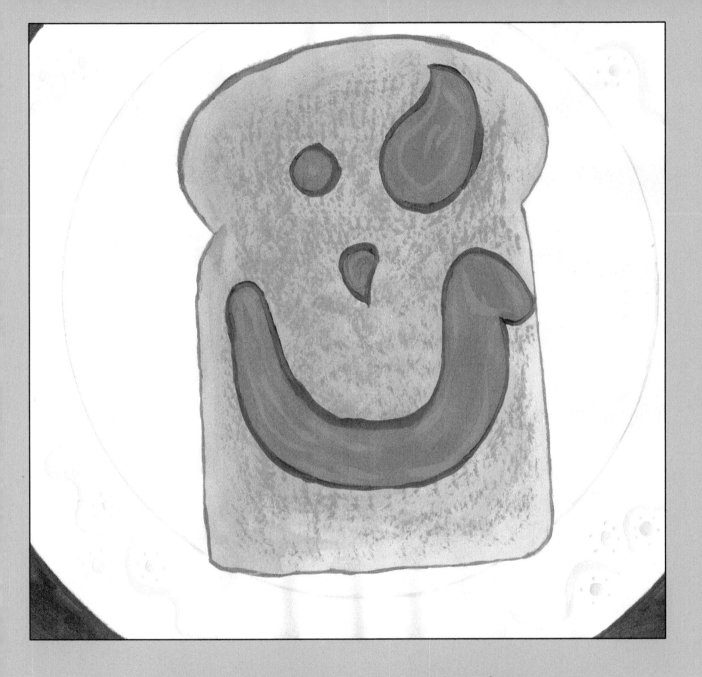

Dr. Mom sees medicine in every situation, including
this poor piece of toast that has a blown pupil.

A curb side consult is often oh, so tempting.

Dr. Mom's life can definitely be chaotic. But imagine a Dr. Mom/Dr. Dad household...

Author and Illustrator Bio

Lauren Hayward is a rural family physician in Listowel, Ontario, Canada. She routinely leaves her car keys in the ignition and forgets what she had for breakfast. This absent-mindedness has increased since having a baby, so now she usually puts her keys in the fridge instead. She is, however, excellent at falling asleep during movies and burning baked goods. She is the co-creator of her son, Alistair. When she is not seeing patients, charting or looking for things she has misplaced, she can be found enjoying the outdoors with her family and friends, travelling, and attempting new recipes that she is hopeful she may not burn. She lives with her husband Jeremy, Alistair, and their super hairy but cuddly dogs, Jack and Jill.

Cheryl Souch is the middle child of the Darlows. She has lived on a farm for most of her life. She has six children and no medical experience besides patching up boo-boos. She loves trying new things, which sometimes gets her into trouble. She has a huge love for nature, the outdoors and camping in the bush.